A GIFT FOR:

_____

FROM:

_____

For every child who has fallen asleep on Christmas Eve, dreaming of Santa . . .

The Night Before CHRISTMAS

The Night Before Christmas
Written by Clement C. Moore
Illustrated by Scott Gustafson

Copyright 2005 by Ariel Books
This edition published under license from Ariel Books, exclusively by Hallmark Cards, Inc.
All art © by Scott Gustafson, and licensed by Ariel Books.

Visit Hallmark on the Web at www.Hallmark.com.
ISBN: 1-59530-105-4
BOK6052

The Night Before CHRISTMAS

WRITTEN BY Clement C. Moore

ILLUSTRATED BY Scott Gustafson

GIFT BOOKS
from Hallmark

INTRODUCTION

With visions of sugarplums dancing in their heads, millions of children all over the world go to bed on Christmas Eve in excited anticipation of the long-awaited visit from Santa and his eight tiny reindeer.

Written by Clement C. Moore in 1822 and first titled "An Account of a Visit from St. Nicholas," this holiday favorite is said to have been created for Moore's children as a special Christmas treat. It was first read aloud while the children and an assortment of relatives were gathered around the family's fireplace. So delighted were the children by the poem that one of the young relatives took it and submitted it anonymously to the <u>Sentinel</u>, a Troy, New York, newspaper. The paper first published the poem on December 23, 1823.

Since then, "The Night Before Christmas," as it is now most often known, has become a wonderful part of the traditional Christmas celebration. It is a story loved equally by both the young...and the young at heart.

'Twas the night before Christmas, when all through the house
Not a creature was stirring, not even a mouse.
The stockings were hung by the chimney with care,
In hopes that St. Nicholas soon would be there.
The children were nestled all snug in their beds,
While visions of sugarplums danced in their heads.

And Mama in her kerchief, and I in my cap,
  Had just settled our brains for a long winter's nap...
  When out on the lawn there arose such a clatter,
  I sprang from my bed to see what was the matter.
  Away to the window I flew like a flash,
  Tore open the shutters and threw up the sash.
  The moon on the breast of the new-fallen snow
  Gave the luster of mid-day to objects below,
  When, what to my wondering eyes should appear,
  But a miniature sleigh and eight tiny reindeer,

With a little old driver, so lively and quick,

I knew in a moment it must be St. Nick.

More rapid than eagles his coursers they came,

And he whistled and shouted and called them by name:

"Now, Dasher! Now, Dancer! Now, Prancer and Vixen!

On, Comet! On, Cupid! On, Donder and Blitzen!

To the top of the porch! To the top of the wall!

Now dash away! Dash away! Dash away all!"

As dry leaves that before the wild hurricane fly,

When they meet with an obstacle, mount to the sky,

So up to the housetop the coursers they flew,

With the sleigh full of toys, and St. Nicholas, too.

And then, in a twinkling, I heard on the roof
The prancing and pawing of each little hoof.
As I drew in my head and was turning around,
Down the chimney St. Nicholas came with a bound.
He was dressed all in fur, from his head to his foot,
And his clothes were all tarnished with ashes and soot.
A bundle of toys he had flung on his back,
And he looked like a peddler just opening his pack.

His eyes, how they twinkled! His dimples, how merry!
His cheeks were like roses; his nose like a cherry!
His droll little mouth was drawn up like a bow,
And the beard on his chin was as white as the snow.
The stump of a pipe he held tight in his teeth,
And the smoke, it encircled his head like a wreath.
He had a broad face and a little round belly
That shook when he laughed, like a bowl full of jelly.
He was chubby and plump, a right jolly old elf,
And I laughed when I saw him, in spite of myself.

A wink of his eye and a twist of his head
Soon gave me to know I had nothing to dread.
He spoke not a word, but went straight to his work,
And filled all the stockings, then turned with a jerk,
And laying his finger aside of his nose,
And giving a nod, up the chimney he rose.

He sprang to his sleigh, to his team gave a whistle,
And away they all flew like the down of a thistle.
But I heard him exclaim, ere he drove out of sight,
"Happy Christmas to all, and to all a good-night!"

ABOUT THE ARTIST

Scott Gustafson grew up in Marengo, Illinois, and pursued a career in animation at the Chicago Academy of Fine Arts and Columbia College. During his studies, illustrations by N.C. Wyeth, Arthur Rackham, Norman Rockwell, and others helped him realize that fine-art illustration, not animation, offered him the most interesting and artistically rewarding opportunities. His work soon appeared in The Saturday Evening Post and other national publications. Mr. Gustafson has illustrated special editions of The Nutcracker, Classic Fairy Tales, and Peter Pan. He also wrote and illustrated the children's favorites Alphabet Soup and Animal Orchestra.

If your household has enjoyed this book, Hallmark would love to hear from you.
Please send comments to:
Book Feedback
2501 McGee, Mail Drop 215
Kansas City, MO 64141-6580

Or E-mail us at booknotes@hallmark.com

The text of this book is set in
sixteen point Cantor Alternate Text Light PKA
and the display in
twenty-five point Cantor Four Light PKA.